S0-AWN-279

Published and distributed by

ISLAND HERITAGE
P U B L I S H I N G

99-880 IWAENA STREET, 'AIEA, HAWAI'I 96701-3202
PHONE: (800) 468-2800 • FAX: (808) 488-2279
EMAIL: hawaii4u@islandheritage.com

ISBN 0-89610-422-2
First Edition, First Printing – 2001

Copyright ©2001 Island Heritage Publishing All rights reserved.
No portion of this book may be reproduced in whole or in part in
any form or by any means without prior written permission from
Island Heritage Publishing. Printed in China.

Footloose the Mongoose
& His Wonderful 'Ohana

By Elaine Masters   Illustrated by Jeff Pagay

DEDICATION

To all the *keikis* in the world who share their bedrooms with lots of *'ohana*. Elaine Masters

To my wonderful *'ohana*, Mom and Dad, Helen and Larry Pagay. Thanks for all
the encouragement and inspiration! Jeff Pagay

Footloose the Mongoose and his friend Shifty sat outside the little house in the bushes by the big, wide ocean. Footloose played his *'ukulele* and sang. Shifty harmonized. It sounded beautiful.

2

Off in the distance, who should appear but Footloose's uncle and auntie and his five little cousins: Loko, Moko, Spim, Spam, and their sister, Pukalani.

Footloose's father called out, "Hey, brah, you visiting or what?"

His brother dropped his heavy load. "Maybe more than visiting.

A bulldozer smashed our house. We got no place to stay."

Uncle and Auntie and their five children, Loko, Moko, Spim, Spam and Pukalani looked sad and worried.

"Of course you must stay with us," said Footloose's father. "By and by, we'll dig some extra rooms for you."

"Yes," said Footloose's mother. "And until then, all your children can sleep with Footloose. You're family. You're *'ohana.*"

Now it was Footloose who looked sad and worried!

The cousins followed Footloose to his room. Loko, Moko, Spim, and Spam dumped their stuff in the middle of the floor. It blended well with Footloose's treasures.

But Pukalani took one look at the messy room and stuck up her nose. "Pilau!" she said. "What a stinky, awful bedroom. I won't stay here." She turned and marched down the hall, taking her bundle with her.

The boys didn't call her back.

Everyone in the 'ohana slept well that night. Everyone except Footloose. When he turned on his left side, WHAM! Loko's shoulder bumped his nose. When he turned on his right side, WHACK! Moko's elbow banged his eye. When he lay on his back, WHOMP! Spim's leg slapped his stomach. And Spam? He snored so hard the whole bed shook.

Poor Footloose. By morning, he was more tired than when he went to bed.

He packed his bag and went to Shifty's. He always liked to visit Shifty's family. Their whole house was just like his bedroom. Messy.

"My mother says we're all 'ohana," Footloose told his friend. "But we're an awfully big 'ohana."

"Sounds like too much 'ohana," agreed Shifty. "Come, have some breakfast with me."

After a yummy breakfast of earthworms sprinkled with chopped beetles, Footloose felt encouraged. "Let's go ask Mrs. Honu what to do about my great big 'ohana," said Footloose.

So they trotted down to the beach. But Mrs. Honu had taken her class on a field trip and was nowhere to be seen.

Footloose pointed to something across the water. "What's that?" he asked.

"Another island," said Shifty. "I've never been there, but it doesn't look too far. I think if we both paddled we could make it."

"Paddled?" asked Footloose.

"Don't you remember? My family has a canoe," said Shifty. "Let's take a little vacation to that island. I think that's just what you need."

"Hmm, I don't know. Maybe I should ask my mother," said Footloose.

"Nah," said Shifty. "With all that *'ohana*, she won't miss you. Come on. The water is so calm today, we won't even get seasick."

Carefully, they stepped into the canoe. Shifty paddled. Footloose paddled.
They paddled a long, long time.

At last they reached the island. It was beautiful, with high mountains and a waterfall that came right down to the beach.

"Come on," said Shifty. "That looks like a cave over there."

They dragged the canoe up on the shore. They scampered off to explore the cave, staying near the entrance where there was still a little light.

Then they splashed in the waterfall, and rolled in the sun-warmed grass to dry off.

Back on the beach, Shifty said, "These shells look different. Let's take some home to old Mrs. Honu." So they filled up their pockets.

"We really should be starting back," Footloose said. "I think it's *kau kau* time." He was talking about dinner, but really he was thinking about his father and mother. What were they doing? Had they missed him? Were they worried? And those cousins—what if his parents started to like Loko, Moko, Spim, Spam, and Pukalani more than they liked him? He really did need to get home.

"I don't like the looks of that sky," said Shifty,

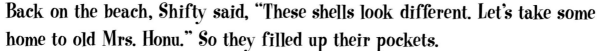

18

staring at some big, black storm clouds. "This channel can get awfully choppy in rough weather."

The two mongooses paddled with all their strength, but they couldn't outrace the storm. Waves tossed the canoe to and fro. Footloose was afraid they might capsize, *huli* right over.

Soon Shifty was too seasick to help, but Footloose paddled on. His arms were so tired they burned like fire. But the canoe didn't seem to be moving any closer to shore.

"Can we help you?" A familiar voice caroled from the water.

It was old Mrs. Honu and her turtle class!

"Toss the rope overboard," she instructed. "We'll pull you along."

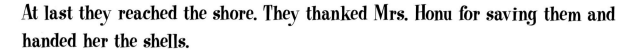

At last they reached the shore. They thanked Mrs. Honu for saving them and handed her the shells.

"My goodness, these are lovely," she said. "I'll add them to the counting shells at school. Now, you boys best be getting home."

They waved goodbye. Shifty trotted off through the rain to his house. Footloose trotted the other way to his house.

His mother greeted him at the door. "Oh, I'm so glad you're safe," she said. "It's quite a storm we're having. But now that you're home, our 'ohana is all snug and secure. Did you have a nice day playing with Shifty?"

Footloose nodded and gave his mother a big hug. He decided to keep quiet about canoes and islands.

He was delighted to find that Father and Mother, Uncle and Auntie had dug out new rooms. Now Uncle and Auntie could share a room. Loko, Moko, Spim, and Spam would share a room. And Pukalani had a room all to herself.

And once again, so did Footloose.

He flopped down in the middle of his bed to take a nap. He was so tired.

He lay on his right side, but he couldn't sleep. He lay on his left side, but he couldn't sleep. Then he lay on his back, but he still couldn't sleep. He was too lonely!

He got up and strummed his *'ukulele*. A tune ran around in his head, and soon he had words to go with the tune. He practiced and practiced.

It was a good song. It was so good, he wanted to share it.

"I know what I'll do," said Footloose.

He dug a hole in his floor and tunneled off to one side. Soon he popped up in the middle of his boy cousins' room. Were they surprised!

Loko, Moko, Spim, and Spam were excited about the
secret tunnel. They zipped back to Footloose's
room to hear the new song. They began to
sing along.

30

"Dinner's ready," Pukalani called from the kitchen. "I fixed my specialty: spider stew."

Spider stew! Footloose's favorite. He decided there wasn't *too* much 'ohana after all. It was a wonderful *'ohana*—just right!

IN CASE YOU'RE WONDERING

In Hawai'i, *'ohana*, family, is very important. Many human families – as well as mongoose families – live together in extended quarters, adding a room here and there as needed. On weekends, the beaches are filled with three- or even four-generation families – barbecuing, surfing, splashing in the ocean, talking story, minding the babies, and playing *'ukulele*.

The word *'ohana* implies more than meets the eye, however. It also includes distant relatives and *hānai* (informally adopted) members, as well as deceased ancestors: the whole family tree.

'Ohana is so important that parts of the family are named after parts of the *kalo*, or taro plant, the traditional food staple of the Hawaiians. A human parent is called a *makua*, the main stalk of a *kalo* plant. A child is a sprout, or *'ohā*. An extended family is an *'ohana*, like the off-shoots of a *kalo* plant. Some people say that *'ohana* may also have the word *hā* tucked inside. *Hā* means breath – and Footloose the Mongoose would agree that family is truly the breath of life.

THE END

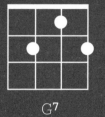
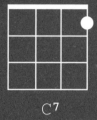
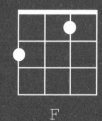

G⁷   C⁷   F

ISLAND HOPPING
by Jeff Pagay

INTRO G⁷ C⁷ F G⁷ C⁷ F

F
It's so nice to get away

C⁷   F
For a week or for a day

F
Cross the ocean big and blue

C⁷   F
with a friend in my canoe.

G⁷ C⁷ F G⁷ C⁷ F

F
Going places that are new

C⁷   F
Lots to see and lots to do

F
Trav'ling's nice but when we're through

C⁷   F
It's nice returning home to you

G⁷ C⁷ F G⁷ C⁷ F

PAU